ISA'S FIRST FAST

A Book of Choices

Written by: Hira Rizvi
Illustrated by: Nida Syed

Copyright © 2020 by Zair Zabr Play

All rights reserved. No part of this book may be reproduced or used in any manner without written permission of the copyright owner except for the use of quotations in a book review. For more information, address: zairzabrplay@gmail.com

FIRST EDITION

www.zairzabrplay.com

Acknowledgment

This wouldn't be possible without Allah who is the best of planners. He gave me the luxury of having the time to pursue my passion.

My husband - who has supported me in more ways that can be listed.

My family - my mom, dad, sisters (of all kinds) and brother - for giving me the experiences and values that shape my outlook in life

My muses - my daughter, niece and nephews - and all the little Muslims out there navigating this big world!

Table of Contents

The Stars	1
A Visitor	7
Suhoor	15
Sleep takes over	20
The Idea	25
Candies for a Cause	30
Payback	37
For Charity	45
Plan B	51
Just a Bite	59
Not even water?	63
Basketball	68
Dribble Left, Dribble Right	75
New Game Strategy	83
The Mosque	90

Candies for Wudu   97

The Confession   105

Welcome to Isa's world. He lives at home with his mom, Mama, and a dad, Baba, who love him dearly.

This Ramadan, Isa is about to fast for the first time. He will still have to go to school where most of his friends don't know much about Ramadan. Isa is afraid they might not understand.

At the end of some of the chapters, you will see two choices. Help Isa out by making choices throughout his day.

The Stars

Tomorrow is the day, thought Isa, lying on his bed while bouncing a ball against the ceiling of his room. Tomorrow would be the first day of Ramadan and Isa's first year fasting. He had known this day was coming for almost a year and had spent months preparing for it. Up until yesterday Isa had been really excited about fasting. He loved all the attention his mom and dad were giving him. A few days back, the whole family went to pick out some of Isa's all time favorite foods to have for Ramadan.

Still, he couldn't help but feel nervous. Isa's stomach was in all kinds of weird knots.

"Isa! Come downstairs!" his mom called up. The nervousness was weighing on him so much that he could hardly pick up his feet. It was as if the knots from his stomach had crawled down to his legs and tied them together.

He was so tired! How could he possibly go through the day without any food or water? Isa had been counting the hours between sunrise and sunset multiple times. It was nearly fifteen hours! He couldn't think straight with all these crazy thoughts zooming through his head.

"Ughh, what is it, Mama?" Isa asked, floating downstairs - still lost in his thoughts. He was so preoccupied with how he would make it through the day tomorrow that he didn't notice where he was going.

He turned the corner and stopped in his tracks. Had the mere thought of not eating gotten to his head? He could hardly believe his eyes.

"What happen-" he tried to blurt out, rubbing his eyes.

Their living room had been transformed! Everywhere Isa looked he saw stars twinkling. Isa was in awe. His jaw dropped and his eyeballs felt like they would fall out of their sockets. It was still dark outside so the lights shone brighter than he had ever seen.

Isa glided through the downstairs area. It was still his house with the same couch, the same TV, and the same people, but it was as if the air had been sucked out and replaced with something spectacular. There was peace and wonder in the air.

He traced his fingers along the mantle where a garland of star lights was tangled with a banner spelling out R-a-m-a-d-a-n.

At the foot of the fireplace was a stack of new books all about Ramadan. Isa bent down and started to look through them. He couldn't help but smile. The books brought back fond memories of him snuggling with his Mama and Baba as they read to him.

"Like it?" Mama asked. "I wanted to make our house extra special this year. Want to know why?" Isa rolled his eyes as he got up and walked into the kitchen.

"It's your first time fasting, and I know you are going to make us so proud," Mama continued as she followed him into the kitchen. "I can still remember my first fast in Pakistan. My mom, your Nani, got up extra early to make my favorite foods for Suhoor! We had a giant party that night. I am so excited to celebrate your fast now! Because you know..."

"I know, I know, because my first fast is a once in a lifetime kind of thing," he interrupted in a robotic tone.

Why did she have to remind me? I was finally not thinking about fasting, Isa thought, annoyed, as the knots in his stomach returned.

The kitchen had also received a Ramadan makeover. Mama had replaced all the tea towels with purple ones, and there were lanterns on the kitchen island with candles flickering in the breeze. The breakfast table had lights strung around, giving it a soft glow. Isa was once again lost in awe of it all.

Then he saw the sign: "Suhoor 4:55 AM, Iftaar 8:07 PM." Isa couldn't help but let out a giant groan as he was reminded about tomorrow's fast.

That's when he noticed something, or rather some*one*, out of the corner of his eye. Humza? What was he doing here? Right now?

A Visitor

"Look who came to see you," Mama said when she noticed Isa looking towards Humza. "I guess he's here to wish you luck for tomorrow!"

"Humza! What are you doing here?" Isa asked. Eager to be distracted from the thought of fasting, he grabbed Humza's hand and said, "Let's go upstairs and play video games!"

"No can do, Isa, I'm here on official mosque business," Humza said matter-of-factly. "We need to discuss the big carnival." he continued, guiding Isa back into the living room.

"Sorry Aunty, official youth cabinet members only for this meeting," he told Mama as he blocked her from following them.

"So are we all set for the party at the mosque tomorrow night?" Isa asked, sinking into the couch. Isa and Humza were part of the youth committee at their local mosque. Humza was the president and Isa was the treasurer.

They met every Sunday and were allowed to plan fun things that kids *actually* wanted to do. Last month they had organized a movie night in the parking lot. Sheraz had borrowed his dad's projector, and they watched the latest Avengers movie under the stars.

The best part of the youth committee was the fact that the kids had full control. Adults had a way of taking something that was supposed to be fun and just ruining it! *Everything* somehow turned into homework or a test, or worse, a teachable moment, blegh! Brother Hashim was the only grown-up that was allowed, though only because he was actually a kid at heart.

Tomorrow night was going to be the biggest event the youth committee had ever done. They had been raising money for it for almost a year!

They had planned a giant carnival to celebrate the first fast. But what made this carnival different was there were going to be real prizes, not just a lollipop. That's right. People would actually get to win a prize that was not candy. It was going to be revolutionary. That was why Humza was here. They had to decide how many prizes to buy.

"So tell me again, what's the total we raised?" Humza asked.

"$3,250," Isa replied.

"Are you sure? Do you want to go and double-check?" Humza questioned.

"Of course I'm sure! I am the treasurer, remember?" Isa blurted louder than he had meant to. Isa was growing impatient with the conversation because it was just reminding him about fasting.

"All right, all right...if you say so" Humza said defensively. "Then I'm going to place an order for the prizes tonight!"

"Great," muttered Isa with his arms folded. He was lost in his own thoughts again. The knots were back. "I guess I'll see you tomorrow night, hungry and thirsty," said Isa in a snarky voice.

"You know, if you stop focusing on all the bad things about fasting, you might notice some great perks, like that awesome hot chocolate station your mom set up for you in the kitchen," Humza said as he walked out the door.

Isa stomped up the stairs, feeling the weight of each step as he went. "Perks!" he mumbled. *What perks? Being hungry? I don't understand why Humza isn't more upset about fasting!* he thought to himself. Isa opened the drawer of his desk and pulled out the youth committee safety box and slammed it on his desk.

Even though he was 150% positive that it was exactly $3,250, he figured there was no harm in counting it one more time.

"...three $20 bills mean $60 so all together it's..."

Isa's heart dropped down to the floor, through the living room, and all the way to the basement. Time stood still.

"...$3,060...." He had remembered wrong. Or maybe he had counted wrong the first time. Or maybe he'd misplaced the bills.

Isa started to frantically search the safety box,

then his desk drawer, then under his desk, under his bed, under his carpet...anywhere, everywhere! Isa desperately wanted this not to be his fault.

But there were no more bills. He had made a mistake and he was missing almost $200.

He couldn't shake the feeling that someone would find out about his mistake. It was as if dread had been injected into his veins and was spreading through his body.

What was he going to do? He couldn't possibly just call up Humza and tell him! Not after he had snapped at him earlier about recounting the money!

Humza wouldn't understand. Isa would never hear the end of it.

All these thoughts whizzed in his head as he tried to go to bed.

BRIIINGGGGG

Isa's alarm was going off. It was time for Suhoor! He was sure he had *just* fallen asleep! How could it possibly be morning already?

He gazed towards the window and saw it was pitch black outside. *This. is. inhumane.* he thought as he buried his head under the pillow.

Should Isa Wake Up?
Go to page 15: Suhoor

OR

Should he try and catch some sleep before tomorrow?
Go to page 20: Sleep Takes Over

Suhoor

Every inch of Isa's body was screaming to stay in bed where it was warm and cozy, but he knew it wasn't a good idea. Today was going to be hard as it was, skipping Suhoor was just *asking* for trouble!

Isa practically slid off the bed, trying to use as little energy as he could, and made his way to the bathroom. The heat must have been broken because the floor felt like ice as he stepped through the dark hall. Out of the corner of his eye he saw something twinkling; it was the lights Mama had strung up on the staircase. Their gentle flickering lit a path down the stairs where Isa could see the glow from the kitchen. Seeing the lights warmed up Isa enough, and he walked into the bathroom smiling.

As he was brushing his teeth, he heard a distinct whirrrrrr sound. He paused and listened again. Whiirrrrr. There was no mistaking that sound. Isa barely finished brushing his teeth and flew down the stairs. There it was. A glorious stack of pancakes. A set of five pancakes, to be exact, wearing the crown jewel, whipped cream with a strawberry.

"As salamu alaykum," Baba said, smiling while sipping on his chai. "I'm assuming the perks of fasting are a bit more obvious now, huh?"

Isa couldn't even bother with a reply as he pulled the plate closer to him and dug in.

"Ten more minutes to eat," Mama announced as she got up to put her plate in the sink. The pressure was on. Isa still had two of the pancakes to work through and the clock was ticking. It was time to make those bites bigger and faster.

I just need to get the pancakes inside my mouth in the next ten minutes. They never said chewing was not allowed while you fast, reasoned Isa in his head, maneuvering another bite into his mouth.

"You know you don't have to finish all the pancakes, right?" Mama said as she made some hot chocolate.

Isa tried to answer but didn't have the time or space to move his mouth. Just as he was about to position the next bite in his mouth Mama startled him by yelling, "Isa, stop it!"

"You are just going to make yourself sick and end up throwing up," she said as she took Isa's plate away from him. "Suhoor and fasting aren't just about food; fasting is about focusing on Allah."

Isa couldn't help but roll his eyes again. *Of course it's about the food,* he thought. *All the perks are food-related!*

After the family had cleaned up, they gathered

in the living room to pray Fajr, the morning prayers. The main lights were off. There was only a soft glow from the decorative lights Mama had strung up.. The star lights on the mantle flickered in a calm rhythmic pattern, almost as if they were breathing too.

The softness of the prayer rug provided warmth as Isa raised his hands to make a dua. That's when the dread came back.

The memories rushed into his head. Humza in the living room. The carnival. The order for the prizes. The missing $200.

Isa's heart began to race. He couldn't breathe. He was panicking. He had fifteen hours to figure out how to find $200. What was he going to do?

Just as these thoughts were clouding his head, Baba started reciting the Quran and his voice drowned out all the other thoughts and calmed Isa down.

"...And Allah is the Best of Planners..." Baba recited.

Isa took a deep breath and prayed that in the morning Allah would show him how to come up with the missing $200, preferably without telling anyone.

> *Go to page 25:*
> *The Idea*

Sleep takes over

At this point, sleep is more important than food, Isa thought to himself. *No amount of food could make up for not having slept.* He could hear clinks and clanks from the kitchen.

"Isa! Come on! You'll run out of time," Mama called out again.

Isa grabbed his ball and threw it at the door to shut it. He pulled his covers over his head and sank a little deeper into his bed.

He sighed and let sleep take over his body

once again.

"ISA!!" Mama yelled. Isa woke up to everything shaking, he was convinced that there was an earthquake! *It must be a big one*, Isa thought as he jumped out of bed and landed with his two feet apart, arms ready to deflect anything coming at him. He looked around his room and reality hit him. Mama was standing in front of him with her arms crossed.

There was definitely no earthquake. By the look on her face, Isa was in big trouble.

"What are you doing? You scared me half to death," Isa said, pulling at his comforter as he tried to climb back into bed.

"Did you not hear me call you downstairs a million times for Suhoor?" Mama asked, pulling the covers off again.

"I did. I wasn't hungry" Isa said sheepishly as he turned over so his back was to her. He closed his eyes, trying to fall back asleep. He felt guilty ignoring her but he really wanted to sleep.

"Well, time for Suhoor is done, go do wudhu - it's time for Fajr prayers," Mama said, disappointment apparent in her voice. She flicked on the lights as she left the room; the lights were so bright that he could see them through his closed eyelids.

GROWL ... his stomach grumbled. Isa realized he actually was hungry. He flipped over and held his stomach and tried to fall back asleep.

GROWL ... his stomach echoed again. Isa let out a loud sigh as he flung his legs over the side of his bed and sat up.

Fine, he thought to himself, *I might as well go downstairs and pray Fajr if my stomach isn't going to let me sleep.*

Isa tugged his shirt sleeves down, trying to cover his hands. It was so cold in the mornings.

When Isa finally made it downstairs, he noticed Mama and Baba had gathered to pray in the living room.

He noticed the skillet still on the counter with a bag of chocolate chips. *I wonder if they had pancakes this morning,* Isa thought, glancing longingly at the kitchen. Pancakes were his absolute favorite food. Especially when Mama stacked them up and added whipped cream on top. It was like going to the pancake house, but at home!

As Isa took off his slippers to enter the living room, he noticed two empty mugs on the coffee table. The foam on the mugs was definitely from hot chocolate. *It must have felt so nice and warm,* thought Isa.

GROWL

Isa dragged himself to the prayer mat and began to pray. He couldn't concentrate because he was so hungry. As he raised his hands for dua he suddenly remembered the missing $200.

Dread took over. He tried to concentrate on Baba reading the Quran. His voice usually calmed Isa down, but he couldn't hear anything over his stomach. Isa closed his eyes. He was so frustrated that he wanted to cry. After praying he climbed back into bed, hoping to get some rest. But the thought of the $200 was keeping him up. On top of that, his stomach was growling non-stop. *Today is going to be brutal,* he thought, tossing in his bed.

Isa was still awake when the sun lit up the sky outside his window, yet he couldn't get up. He felt so drained and the day had just begun. How was he going to get through today?

The Idea

Isa was so late! He shoved his math homework into his bag as he ran down the stairs. The math homework had been tough; it had taken him hours to complete.

Dave had come over last week to try and work on it with Isa but they couldn't figure it out. Isa was really proud that he had finished it and wondered how many other kids had solved the problems. It was worth a lot of points.

He walked into the pantry and grabbed a snack for recess before remembering that he was fasting. *That was close,* he thought as he walked out. That's when an idea dawned on him: *Even though I am fasting, none of the other kids are,* thought Isa, smiling to himself.

The hot chocolate station that Mama had set up was stocked with every kind of chocolate, crackers, and treats you could imagine. Isa could take these wonderful treats and sell them during recess to the other kids.

Problem solved, Isa thought as he loaded up the goodies into his bag. And technically, he wasn't stealing any of this. Mama had set all this up for his once-in-a-lifetime fast. He simply was choosing to use it differently than she had intended.

At school, Isa was anxiously waiting for the bell to ring for recess. He wanted to sell the treats so he could finally stop worrying about the $200.

GROWL...he looked down at his book, heat

rushing to his face. He was pretty sure EVERYONE heard his stomach. He was so embarrassed.

RIIINGGG... finally! Recess! Isa rushed outside. He knew exactly where he was going to set up his candy store: under the tree where he and his friends usually ate their snacks. Isa had been working out the pricing in his head when he realized he didn't have a sign. *That's okay* he thought, *no time for it now*, he had to focus on selling as much candy as he could before recess was over.

Dave, Anthony, Shannon, and Sajjad were already gathered under the tree to eat their snacks.

Dave pulled out a gooey strawberry tart.

GROWL - Isa's stomach protested.

Anthony pulled out a smoothie with a side of sliced apples.

Isa's throat got tighter.

Sharon pulled out an M&M yogurt and licked the spoon.

Isa's mouth started to water.

Before Sajjad could pull out his snack, Isa ran back into the classroom. He was drooling!

Isa's stomach gave another growl. This was so much harder than he had imagined. He was so hungry, and seeing everyone's snack made him drool. Isa wrapped his arms around his stomach to try and control the growls. It was almost like someone or something was inside his stomach and pulling it inwards.

He knew he had to go back outside. He had to sell his candy to make $200 for tonight.

Candies for a Cause

I'll stay here while they finish up their snacks. It simply isn't worth the risk, Isa thought to himself. What if he accidentally ate something? All of this would be for nothing.

Mama's voice creeped into his ears. "Once-in-a-lifetime event." He couldn't mess up on his first fast. He would forever be known as the kid that messed up on the first try!

Better safe than sorry, he reassured himself.

Anyway, I need to make a sign and figure out if I even have enough candy to make $200, Isa reasoned.

It usually took everyone fifteen minutes to finish eating their snack, so that's how long he had to figure things out. First, he would make the sign.

He needed an amazing name for his candy store. It needed to be purposeful.

"Candies for a Cause," Isa thought out loud. "I bet I could even get the teachers to buy my candy with that name."

Isa grabbed five pieces of paper and taped them together to make a giant sign. Everyone in the playground needed to see the sign.

 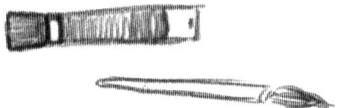 

"Done! And I still have ten minutes left before they are done eating!" Isa said out loud. "Time to make sure I have enough candy to sell to *make* $200!"

As Isa did his calculations, dread started to creep in on him. He didn't have enough candy. He needed a Plan B.

That's when he noticed his math homework sticking out of his bag. Isa began to smile.
Isa wrote, "Meet me in the library before lunch and I will solve all your problems" on pieces of paper.

He couldn't help but chuckle as he tucked them in his friends' notebooks. He felt pretty proud of himself. Maybe his prayers from the morning were finally kicking in. Allah had found a way for him to solve his problem without having to tell Humza that he messed up!

GROWL

Ughh. Just when Isa had almost forgotten about being hungry, his stomach provided a loud reminder of how hungry he was. Isa picked up his candy and shoved it back into his bag.

He walked over to the window to see where everyone was hanging out.

Dave, Anthony, Sharon, and Sajjad were still by the tree, but they weren't eating. They were laughing. They were laughing so hard that they were practically rolling on the ground.

Isa squinted his eyes to see what they were laughing about. Shannon was passing around her phone. Each time one of them looked at it, they burst out into laughter. "There must be a funny picture or something on her phone," Isa mumbled to himself as he put his bag on.

Or...what if they are laughing at me? Is it a picture of me? Isa froze.

What if they saw Isa drool when they took out their snacks earlier? Had Shannon taken a picture of him? What if they shared the picture? What if everyone saw?

They are all laughing at me because I drooled during recess because I'm fasting! Isa's thoughts were whizzing around in his head.

They were so mean! Did they not understand

how hard it already was?

Isa couldn't help but want payback. Maybe if they knew what it was like to be hungry, they'd understand and not laugh.

| Should Isa go outside and sell his candy? Go to page 45: Charity | **OR** | Should Isa get payback and let the other kids know what it feels like to be hungry? Go to page 37: Payback |

Payback

Isa turned around and slid to the floor with his back to the wall. How could they be so insensitive? Isa hadn't told them that he was fasting but they should have noticed that he had not eaten anything all day?

If anything, Sajjad should have told them! How could he stand there and make fun of Isa too! Sajjad knew all about fasting and how hard it was! Sajjad went to the same Sunday school as Isa. He should have explained fasting to the rest of them rather than laughing at Isa's picture.

"Well, maybe it's time I show them what it feels like to fast," Isa mumbled to himself as he got up off the floor. "I'll just sell my candy during lunch," he justified to himself, "this is more important."

Isa slid his bag off his shoulder and started to pace around the room, looking for inspiration. What could Isa do that would force them to feel like he did - hungry? Of course he needed to make sure it couldn't be traced back to him.

As Isa walked between the desks, something caught his eye. It was a bright pink lunch bag sticking out of Amanda's bag.

Isa looked around to make sure no one was looking. He closed the door to the classroom quietly and sat down softly on Amanda's desk.

He gently slid the lunch box out of her bag and opened it. Her mom had packed her pasta, orange slices, a cheese stick and even a little heart chocolate.

Isa's mouth began to drool. Those orange slices looked so juicy and refreshing. Isa's throat had been feeling so dry. He couldn't help but sit and stare down at Amanda's packed lunch longingly.

Isa's plan was to throw out everyone's lunch so they would all be hungry. That way they could feel a little bit of what Isa felt. And then when he would offer them candy, they would drool too!

He grabbed everyone's lunch boxes and made a pile next to the garbage can. He needed to empty them quickly and put them back in their bags before everyone came in from recess.

Just as he was about scrape Amanda's pasta into the garbage, the door opened. Isa jumped and hid the container behind his back. Oh no! He was done for.

"Isa? What are you doing here? Why aren't you outside?"

It was Mr. Kendall. Isa wished it would have been any other teacher but him. Mr. Kendall was the only teacher at the school worth calling "cool." Isa was hoping he would end up in Mr. Kendall's class next year.

Mr. Kendall walked in and noticed Isa's giant sign. "Oh wow, are you raising money for a charity, Isa?"

Isa was really flustered and his stomach gave a loud growl. "Err...yeah! See you later!" Isa tried to run out. He had just made it out the door when he heard Mr. Kendall call him back. He had noticed the pile of lunch boxes next to the garbage can.

When Mr. Kendall asked him to explain, Isa tried to come up with a good cover-up story, but his stomach was growling so much that he couldn't think straight. He ended up telling Mr. Kendall all about his plan to throw out everyone's lunch so they would be hungry. He tried to defend himself by telling Mr. Kendall about everyone laughing at him for drooling.

"Thank you for your honesty Isa, but you know two wrongs don't make a right" Mr. Kendall spoke as he led Isa into his office. Isa was sitting in Mr. Kendall's office with his head bowed down. Mr. Kendall was letting him know that there was a strict school policy about touching other people's things. He had to not only call Isa's mom up and tell her about what had happened, but also suspend him - effective immediately.

Isa was trying to hold back his tears, but they were ready to roll down his face any second. Time seemed to go by so slowly. Isa and Mr. Kendall sat in silence the whole time. He wished he had not been so worried about the other kids, he should have just gone and explained why he had drooled in the first place!

When Mama finally came, she didn't look at Isa. She looked directly at Mr. Kendall and apologized. She walked out of the office without looking back even once to see if Isa was still following her. Mama didn't even glance at Isa once during the whole ride home. Isa followed her inside with his head bowed down low.

Just say something, thought Isa. He could feel her disappointment like needles pricking him through his skin. He didn't even notice that tears had started to roll down his cheeks. He started to make his way upstairs to his room. As he took the first step, Mama finally spoke. "Isa, I think I didn't do a good enough job explaining to you what fasting really means."

Isa stood frozen on the steps. He didn't know

how to respond. Mama sighed and continued, "When you fast, you are supposed to realize how lucky you are to have food every day. How could you even think about throwing away other people's food? I'm really disappointed. You are grounded for the rest of the week. That means you can't go to the carnival tonight."

Isa took a deep breath in and went up to his room and closed the door. How could he have let hunger take over him like that? It had been a monster that clouded his thoughts. That is when Brother Hashim's advice echoed in his head.

"Fasting from food and water is the easy part, but fasting from bad thoughts is harder. Don't lose focus."

Isa had lost focus. Isa had been so worried about what other kids might have been thinking that he forgot to worry about himself. When you are fasting, you are supposed to try and be the best version of yourself - Isa had been the exact opposite.

THE END

For Charity

Breathe in. Step. Breathe out. Step.

Isa was trying to calm down from being upset. He needed to gather courage to sell his candy. He had his sign tucked under one arm and clutched the strap of his bag that held the goods with his other arm.

HAHAHAHAHA. Their laughter was echoing all over the playground. How were they still laughing? *A picture of me drooling isn't* that *funny!* Isa thought in his head.

Eyes on the prize. I just need to have them buy my candy. I need the $200 before we go to the mosque tonight Isa repeated in his head.

"What do you have there, Shannon?" Isa mumbled, staring at the ground. He couldn't bear to look at them when they flipped over the phone to show the picture of him drooling.

"Dude, Isa! You have to check this new app out!" Sajjad blurted, practically jumping over to him. *An app? They were laughing about an app?* Isa was relieved and felt like a weight was lifted off of him. "You can mix your faces together. Look!" Sajjad continued, shoving the phone in front of Isa's face. Even though Isa wanted to scream, he couldn't help but burst out laughing. It was pretty hilarious!

"Hey, what do you have there?" Shannon asked, pointing at the poster tucked under his arm. This was it. This was Isa's moment. He rolled out the sign and taped it to the tree.

"I'm selling candy!" he declared, standing in

front of the tree. He took off his bag and started to lay out all the candy so they could see what he had to offer.

"...for a cause?" Anthony questioned. "As in, you are trying to raise money for a charity?"

Isa panicked. He didn't think about that. Was it wrong for him to say yes? Technically, it was a cause, right? The cause was "help Isa out." And any kind of help was charity, right?

"...uhhh...yeah! For charity!" Isa replied and prayed they wouldn't ask any more questions.

They all gathered around the candy to look at what he had. Isa smiled to himself; finally things were going his way.

Just as quickly as everyone had gathered, they started to back away. "So, do you want to buy any candy?" Isa asked nervously as Anthony turned to leave.

"Well, it's great that you are trying to raise money for charity and all, but I'm not hungry right now," Anthony confessed.

"Yeah, me neither," Shannon said. "I just ate my yogurt, and I'm saving my money to buy lunch in the cafeteria."

Isa's dread was starting to come back, creeping in and spreading all over his body.

Isa was trying to think of what he could say to change their minds but it was so hard. His stomach kept growling and he couldn't even hear his own thoughts. His heart was pounding in his chest. He had to come up with something to say. He needed that money before they went to the mosque tonight.

"ISA!"

Isa snapped back to reality. And the answer had magically appeared in front of him. His heart calmed down and the dread floated away.

Standing in front of him was a line of teachers with full pockets and empty stomachs!

"Would you like to buy some candy?" Isa asked. "It's for charity!" he added.

really are a thoughtful boy, Isa!"

Isa began to beam.

"Wow! You set this up by yourself!" Mr. Hanson said.

Isa was smiling so big his face hurt.

"So what charity are you raising money for?" Mr. Kendall asked, picking up one of the chocolate bars.

Isa's smile dropped. The dread crept in; his heart was racing again. He couldn't confess that there was no real charity. He *had* to come up with a better answer.

"Oh..umm...it's for my mosque!" he lied.

"That's so nice, honey! What are they raising money to do?" Mrs. Bowers inquired.

GROWL. Isa's stomach was picking up again. He was trying so hard to think of the right answer, but he was so hungry.

"...ummm...."

GROWL.

Isa just needed to think.

"Once-in-a-lifetime-" Now Mama's voice was ringing in his head too. It was too much for Isa to handle!

"It's for me, okay!" yelled Isa, louder than he had meant to. His hands clasped on his mouth. All the teachers stopped and looked at him.

"Let's go inside and talk," Mr. Kendall said as he picked up all the candy and walked Isa inside. Isa was in trouble now. Isa was trying really hard to keep tears from rolling down his face. The last thing he needed was everyone to see him crying.

Plan B

Inside Mr. Kendall's office, Isa explained everything that was happening with the youth committee and his plan.

"...and I know it was wrong, and I'm really sorry and it's just really hard to think while I'm fasting, and today is my first day!" Isa ended desperately.

Mr. Kendall took a deep breath and sat back in his chair. "Okay, because you are fasting, and I know it's not easy, I'm going to let this incident slide. A small lie is *still* a lie. You can pick up the candy from my office at the end of the day."

Isa got up to leave Mr. Kendall's office. His heart wasn't pounding in his chest, and there was no dread in his body - it had been replaced by something even worse. He felt embarrassed and ashamed. Mr. Kendall was one of the cool teachers at school, and he had just disappointed him.

"You know, sometimes the easiest choice is the best choice. Maybe letting your youth committee know what really happened and admitting to your mistake is not only easier but will have the best result," Mr. Kendall said. He didn't look up from his computer as Isa slowly walked out of the office.

Back in class, everyone was filing back in from recess and taking their seats. Isa slipped into his seat and buried his head in his arms on his desk.

How many people saw me get into trouble? he wondered.

Isa was thinking about what Mr. Kendall had just said. It was far from easy for Isa to admit he had messed up, especially after the way he had been annoyed with Humza last night. There was nothing easy about telling him that he was right and Isa had miscounted the money. And now Isa's candy was also gone so he couldn't even try to sell it at lunch!

"Psssttt...did you leave this note for me?" Dave whispered. The notes! Isa had totally forgotten about Plan B. There was still hope!

"Yeah, meet me in the library before lunch!" Isa whispered back. "It's a surprise. Spread the word!" Finally, he had a way out of this messy situation! At the library, no one was going to be able to say no to Isa's offer. Isa just hoped enough people would show up so he could raise $200. As soon as the bell for lunch rang, Isa ran to the library and waited for everyone to show up.

"So what's all this about?" Carly asked. Almost the whole class had shown up to hear Isa's offer. The knots in Isa's stomach were back. He couldn't tell if they were there from being hungry or nervous.

"You know the math homework that is due

today? It is worth so many points and it is sooo hard, right?" began Isa.

"Yeah, tell me about it," the crowd agreed.

"Well, I solved all the problems and can solve yours too!" Isa declared, chuckling at his own joke. "If you leave your papers here, I'll finish the assignment during lunch for you."

Anthony and Dave exchanged looks as the crowd fell silent. *They are just stunned,* Isa reassured himself.

"Dude, the homework is due next period, we

finished it already. You should have offered to do it earlier!"

Isa was confused. Earlier? Why didn't he think of that?

"Yeah, plus technically it would be cheating anyway," Amanda said as the crowd turned and walked away. Isa's dread was back and it had company: anger.

Isa was so angry. He was pretty sure his face was red and everyone else could feel the warmth coming off of him!

You know who is to blame here? Mama, fumed Isa in his head. *I bet I would have thought of offering it earlier if I could think straight,* Isa continued. *But I can't think straight because I am fasting and it's a once-in-a-lifetime kind of event!* Isa stomped as his thoughts zoomed about in his head.

Things simply couldn't get worse, until he smelt it.

Coming from the cafeteria was the smell of comfort. It was Pizza Friday. The smell of cheese pizza filled the hallway.

Isa followed the smell till he was standing inside the cafeteria. He was frozen.

He looked to the left and saw Cheryl take a bite of her slice and pull the cheese. It stretched longer and longer, so warm and melty.

James burped loudly as he chugged some cold iced tea. The ice in the cup rattled, drawing more attention to them. The drops of condensation on the bottle confirmed how refreshing that drink must have felt.

GROWL. Isa's stomach spoke up.

GROWL. Isa could hardly stand it anymore.

Anthony walked past him with three slices of pizza piled on his plate, the cheese from each melting into each other.

"Aren't you going to grab a slice?" he asked. No one knew Isa was fasting. What if he cheated just a little?

Should Isa go ahead and grab a slice? Go to page 59: Just a Bite	**OR**	Should he walk away from the cheese? Go to page 63: Not Even Water

Just a Bite

Isa scanned the cafeteria. There was no one there from the mosque and no one there who knew Isa wasn't supposed to be eating. He got in line to grab a slice of pizza. His stomach gave a giant growl. *Patience,* he thought, patting his stomach.

Isa wasn't planning on eating three slices like Anthony; he just wanted to take a couple of bites to help him get through the rest of the day. He was sure *everyone* cheated a little during Ramadan. Fasting seemed more and more impossible the longer the days got.

When the lunch lady placed the slice of pizza on his tray, he could feel the warmth through the plastic on his hand.

GROWL. Was his stomach excited or was it trying to stop him from eating? Either way, there was no turning back now. Isa was doing all he could to hold back his drool.

At the end of the line was the drink station. Isa's mouth started to water again. The cool air from the section felt so refreshing. *Maybe a little drink too*, he thought as he grabbed a cold soda.

Isa didn't even bother putting the drink on his tray; it felt amazing in his hands.

"Isa! Look what I brought for you!" someone called out from behind. It sounded like Sajjad. Sajjad went to the same Sunday school as Isa. He knew Isa was supposed to be fasting. He also knew that fasting meant Isa wasn't supposed to be eating.

Isa started to panic. What if he saw him with the tray of food? Would he tell everyone at the mosque?

Isa pretended not to hear him and walked away quickly.

Thump thump thump. Oh no! Sajjad was following him!

Isa was backed into a corner. He had no choice but to turn around and say, "Hey Sajjad!"

"Dude, I've been calling you for so long. Didn't you hear me?" Sajjad said, panting and trying to catch his breath. "Anyway, I know lunch is going to be hard and really tempting with it being pizza and—"

Sajjad finally looked up and saw that Isa was standing there with a tray of food. He looked so confused. Isa's mind was racing; he needed to come up with a good explanation ASAP.

Now Isa was panting, his heart was pounding, and he felt as if his sneakers were glued into place.

"Aren't you fasting?" Sajjad asked confused.

"I was..." Isa mumbled, he was scared he'd tear up now. "I mean I am...but I just can't do it. I'm so hungry."

Surprisingly, Sajjad smiled and took the tray from Isa's hand. He explained how he had done some practice fasts last year in the winter and lunchtime had been the hardest. That's why he was looking for him!

Isa let out a sigh of relief. He was so glad he hadn't taken a bite. All of this morning would have been for nothing. He was grateful that Sajjad had checked in on him.

Not even water?

The temptation was impossible to ignore. "Once-in-a-lifetime" echoed in Isa's head. He sighed. He thought back to those stories about Ramadan Mama used to read to him growing up. They always had the same message: fasting is a gift from Allah. Fasting allows us to focus on what is important: helping others and giving back to those in need. Fasting allows us to remember those less fortunate than us.

Isa sniffed. He'd been so worried about the

$200 that he had lost sight of why he was fasting in the first place.

Isa slid into the seat next to Anthony at the table. "Bro, you didn't grab a slice. It's like the best pizza ever."

"I can't," Isa explained. "I'm fasting."

"Fasting? What's that?" Dave asked between his bites.

"I can't eat or drink anything between sunrise and sunset," Isa said, looking up at everyone cautiously.

"Not even water?" Shannon was shocked.

"Wait, like ever? But you used to eat," Anthony pointed out.

"Not forever, just for the month of Ramadan. It's actually a really special time for Muslims." Isa gestured to Sajjad for some backup.

"It's really, really hard actually, I couldn't do it, I'm going to try for the first time this weekend," Sajjad added.

Talking about it with his friends somehow made his hunger not feel like such a big deal to Isa. He felt calmer, and the smell of the pizza wasn't bothering him as much.

"So tell me more! How long is Rama-" Sharon stumbled trying to remember the pronunciation. Isa's face beamed. He couldn't believe his friends were actually interested in Ramadan! They were all so impressed and curious.

Isa started to explain to his friends about Ramadan. He told them about the lunar calendar and how it was shorter than the regular calendar, which is why each year Ramadan came at a different time.

"And we actually stay up to see if the moon comes out to find out if it'll be the new month. We camp out in the backyard as a family and drink hot chocolate!" Isa told them.

"That is so cool! It's like you guys have monthly camping trips!" Dave pointed out.

It WAS really cool - the traditions built around their holidays. He started to think about all the effort his mama had put into decorating their house.

"...you might notice some perks." Humza's words rang in Isa's head. Isa made a pledge to himself that from now on he would try and enjoy the moment.

GROWL. Even if his stomach had other plans. After all, today was special, a once-in-a-lifetime kind of special. And he had the carnival at the mosque to look forward to. At that moment, Isa felt proud to be fasting. It takes great strength to say no to all the temptations. He silently thanked Allah for making hims strong enough to fast.

Basketball

"Earth to Isa!" Anthony said, waving his hands in front of Isa's face. Isa must have zoned out thinking about Ramadan. "Oh...uh...yeah?" Isa blurted out.

"Are you ready for basketball?" Anthony asked. Everyone had finished eating and was putting away their trays. "Did you say basketball?" Isa perked up. Things were definitely looking up now!

Basketball was Isa's thing. No one could deny that Isa was the best basketball player at their school. He had been playing basketball as far back as he could remember. He got his first basketball hoop when he was only a year old. Every time his father flipped through the pictures from his first birthday, he always stopped at the picture of Isa unwrapping that present. There was a look of true love on his face!

He was so good that Dave and Anthony actually argued everyday about whose team Isa was going to play on. Isa wondered if that was what it felt like to be a professional NBA player where the big teams drafted players and bid on them.

Truth be told, Isa dreamed of being a professional NBA player. He wouldn't have to worry about school or homework or whether he actually understood algebra or not. He would get to do what he loved, playing basketball, and nothing else.

I wonder what Muslim basketball players do during Ramadan, Isa thought to himself as he followed everyone outside. He'd heard of Enes Kanter, who was a Muslim Turkish-born professional basketball player. The playoffs one year had been at the same time as Ramadan and Isa remembered hearing in the news how Enes Kanter had fasted through it all.

Isa figured maybe it was the stronger players that fasted during Ramadan. Whatever it was, Isa promised himself he would never miss a fast because of a game.

Out on the basketball court, teams had been made and were huddled as they came up with a game plan. The sun was shining down from a cloudless sky. There was humidity in the air too.

Isa's throat felt dry. He swallowed a couple of times to try and relieve some of the scratchiness. Since Isa was on Dave's team, Anthony got Raj on his team. Raj was really good at shooting from afar. He had once made a basket from the half-court line! Everyone who had been watching and playing had let out gasps of amazement. It was awesome!

The teams huddled trying to figure out who

should block Raj and who should be the main shooter. As their shoulders touched, Isa realized how hot it was. Everyone's backs were already drenched in sweat and the game hadn't even begun.

"All right, I think our best bet is Meghan covering Raj. She is the best defense player we've got," Dave dictated to the team.

Sweat started to roll down Isa's face.

"Isa, bro, we are depending on you to make those baskets. You are our secret weapon!" Dave said, pointing at him.

Beads of sweat rolled down to his lips, teasing him.

"LET'S GO!" The team broke off. Isa lifted his shirt to wipe off all the sweat from his face but it wasn't much help. It was so hot that even his shirt was covered in sweat.

Out of the corner of his eye he saw everyone grabbing cups of water.

His mouth began to water again. It was so hot

the sweat was coming into his eyes and blurring his vision.

It was 1 PM meaning Isa couldn't eat or drink anything for another seven hours. On normal days, Isa would pack an extra snack and drink for after the game. He remembered the one time he had forgotten, he had to go to the nurse's office. They said he was dehydrated.

He knew the smarter decision would be to sit out but Dave had fought so hard to have him on his team! Maybe he could play but just go slow?

| Should Isa play but take it slow? Go to page 75: Dribble Left, Dribble Right | **OR** | Should he sit this one out? Go to page 83: New Game Strategy |

Dribble Left, Dribble Right

Isa could definitely take it a little slow - pace himself, not get too tired! It wouldn't be fair to the team if he sat out. Isa lifted his arms over his head and reached over to give it a stretch but he was sweating so much his elbow kept slipping.

He started to jog in place to warm up instead. Isa's sweat was pouring down his face and he couldn't see. He looked around and saw everyone taking a drink.

"Today is supposed to be the hottest it has ever been," Dave reported back as he used his shirt to fan his body.

"Oh yeah?" Isa asked. Maybe it wasn't such a great idea to play.

Isa was starting to doubt his decision, but before he could really think about it, Dave jumped up and slapped Isa on his back and said, "Yeah, but nothing stops us, right?"

"Hah. Yeah, that's right." Isa raised his hand to give a thumbs-up but his arms felt like there were weights attached to them. Isa was truly torn on what he should be doing. He tried to think back on some advice he had gotten.

At the mosque, the youth committee had a big buddy program that Isa was part of. Everyone was paired with an older kid who could answer their questions.

Isa's big buddy was Ayaan. He was so excited when he had found out Ayaan was his big buddy because Ayaan was on the high school basketball team. They were so good they got to go on an overnight tournament in Washington, DC. Ayaan was applying for basketball scholarships for college.

During their last meeting, Ayaan had given Isa a lot of advice. Isa had asked him how he planned to play basketball during Ramadan.

"It's not easy. Now I make sure to have a really good Suhoor so I have energy throughout the day but the key is to pace yourself. My first couple of years fasting I actually sat out most of the games unless they were at night after Iftaar," Ayaan had explained.

I need to pace myself this Ramadan, Isa thought. *Should I sit this game out?* He questioned his decision again. That's when Dave gestured for him to join the rest of the team on the basketball court. Isa could do it. After all, Ayaan played basketball now, right? *I just need to pace myself in this game, go slow,* he told himself.

The game was on. Dribble to the left, dribble to the right, pass the ball to Jonathon, sneak behind Raj, receive and shoot!

YES! Isa scored the first basket of the game! His team rushed over to him and lifted him up! As soon as they did that, Isa felt a little dizzy. He ignored it; he was enjoying the moment.

He was pumping his fist in the air. Woo hoo! Woo hoo! Woo......

Something was happening. Isa couldn't see anymore. Slowly, everyone's cheers started to fade away. All Isa could hear was the sound of his own breathing. There were stars glistening in his eyes. Isa felt something cold on his forehead. The stars came into focus. They were the lights on the mantle... in his living room in his house? What was he doing home? Isa tried to sit up when Mama gently pushed him back down.

"Shhh...try and rest, Isa," she whispered.

"What happened?" Isa asked when he finally

found his voice back.

"Honey, you fainted. You got dehydrated while playing basketball in the hot sun," Mama explained, handing Isa a glass of water.

Fainted? Isa tried to process this in his head. And why was she giving him water, he was fasting! Isa tried to give the water back to her.

"Your fast doesn't count anymore if you are sick. We can try again tomorrow but you have to pace yourself. For now, just try and rest," Mama said as she walked out.

"Wait, what about tonight?" Isa asked weakly. "What about the carnival?"

Mama looked at Isa and sat back down next to him. "It's okay. I'll send the money with Baba to the mosque. Here, why don't you call Humza and let him know."

As Isa sat there with the phone in his lap, he wished he had just told Humza the truth all along. Isa took a deep breath and called Humza.

"Hello?" Humza picked up right away.

"Hey, salam, it's me Isa," he said weakly.

"Oh hey! Are you ready for tonight? How was your first fast?" Humza asked excitedly.

Isa's eyes started to water. He tried his hardest to keep his voice steady as he explained to Humza what had happened at the basketball game and how he couldn't make it.

Humza understood, and reassured Isa that everything would be fine, and that he should focus on resting. Isa was about let out a sigh of release when Humza added -

"Just send the money with your dad, or I can

come pick it up."

Isa sat silently on the other line for a little while, before finally speaking up. He explained to Humza how he must have miscalculated and they were short $200. Now it was Humza who sat silently on the phone.

"You should have just been honest with last night, now I need to call Br. Hashim and figure this out, it would have been so much easier if you told me before."

Isa could feel Humza's frustration through the phone. He tried to explain to him how he had been embarrassed and thought Humza would have been mad and not understood.

"I don't understand" Humza replied "I guess you don't trust me. I'm upset now, because friends don't lie to each other."

Isa felt horrible. He had not only disappointed his friends, but himself too. He had known better.

THE END

New Game Strategy

Who was he kidding? Isa knew himself. He wouldn't be able to take it slow. Especially not after Dave had called him the secret weapon! No way!

"Hey Dave, I'm not sure it's such a great idea for me to play…" Isa confessed. "It's really hot, and you know I can't drink anything till sunset and that's still like seven hours away."

Isa felt crummy letting his team down, but he *really* didn't want to risk not completing his first fast. Especially after he'd made it this far into the day! Isa got ready for Dave to be really annoyed with him.

"Isa! Why didn't you say so before, dude!" Dave exclaimed. "Yo Anthony! We have a problem," he called out across the court. Isa explained the situation to everyone and they decided the best thing to do was to pick the teams again and have Isa be the referee.

Even though it wasn't as fun as playing, being a referee definitely had its perks. Isa was able to observe everyone and see how they played. Now he would be even better on the court. Isa was feeling so good after lunch that he swore his stomach didn't growl once. He finally felt like he was getting used to fasting. The rest of the day seemed to whiz by. Before he knew it, he was on the bus home.

"Isa, try and finish up your homework early today. We have to go to the mosque tonight!" Mama called out as he walked in the front door.

GROWL. His stomach reminded him about his problems - most related to the mosque.

Isa dragged his bag up the stairs. At each step,

the bag made a thumping sound that echoed in the house. He just realized none of his plans to come up with $200 had worked. At the mosque, Humza and Brother Hashim were going to pester him endlessly for the money.

Maybe he should just call Humza now and say it was stolen. *Yeah! That's what I'll do. I'll stage a robbery. Someone stole the $200,* Isa planned in his head.

Isa's story had to be airtight. He needed to know all of the details. Getting caught in a lie would only make all of this ten times worse. Isa started to practice his script.

"So I came home, and my room was a mess. Someone had messed up my bed and thrown my books to the floor. I got so scared and didn't know what had happened. And then I saw it. My—no, our—safety box was open...wide open! I freaked out and counted the money right away. And that's when I realized some of it was missing."

Isa stood silently for a second. *That sounded good*, he thought, nodding to himself. He practiced one more time before gathering his courage to go downstairs and call up Humza.

He kept going over the script in his head as he walked downstairs to borrow Mama's phone. As she handed over her phone, Isa hesitated.

"Isa, are you going to use the phone or not?" asked Mama. Isa had been frozen in the moment and was just holding the phone. What if Humza asked to talk to Isa's parents? Would they call 911?

This lie could spread and blow up really easily. "No thanks," Isa mumbled as he ran back upstairs to his room and closed the door behind him.

Isa sunk to the floor with his back still against the door. *Great, back to square one,* he thought. *Now what?*

He felt doomed. The sky was getting darker and darker with every minute that passed. His chest felt so tight, like it was squeezing his heart. Isa closed his eyes, threw his head back, and took a deep breath. He prayed the answer would magically appear in front of him. And it did. Peeking out of his bag was the candy that Mr. Kendall had confiscated earlier in the day. Isa smiled as an idea dawned on him. He could raise the $200 right at the mosque!

"It's all about learning from your mistakes, right?" he said to himself as he picked up the bag of candy. "Why didn't the kids want to buy the candy during recess? Because they had already eaten!" Iftaar at the mosque wasn't till *after* Maghrib, which meant during prayer time everyone would be hungry! All Isa had to do was sneak the candy into the mosque, sneak out during Maghrib prayer, and find a good spot to sell them his candy. The plan was foolproof.

"Isa, Humza is on the phone, come get it,"

Mama called out from the foot of the stairs. Isa groaned as he went downstairs. He didn't want to talk to Humza till he had the money!

"Hey Salam! How was your first fast?" Humza asked on the phone.

"Fine. Fine. It was just fine. What is it?" Isa spat back a little too angrily. He didn't mean to sound so annoyed, but he really didn't want to talk about the carnival.

"Umm...okay. Well, I just was calling to remind you to bring the mon-" Humza continued.

"Yeah, I know! I am the treasurer. Don't you think I'm responsible enough?" As the words were leaving Isa's mouth, he was regretting them immediately. He was so rude to Humza that he couldn't blame Humza for being mad at him. He definitely couldn't tell him the truth now. He wished he had just been a little nicer.

"Part of fasting is controlling your anger and being patient," Mama said, raising an eyebrow as Isa handed back the phone to her.

The Mosque

As Baba was pulling into the mosque's parking lot, Isa peered outside to see the carnival being set up. He smiled and felt proud of the youth committee. They had been working so hard to plan this event because it truly was a special year for them. This year nearly ten kids, including Isa, were fasting for the first time. Everyone wanted to make sure that this day truly felt like a once-in-a-lifetime kind of milestone. Because it truly was. As the day was ending Isa felt excited and proud of having fasted all day. He recalled the shocked faces of his friends when he had told them about it. It really wasn't easy, but the pride that filled his chest from accomplishing it made it all worth it.

Stepping out of the car, the smell of samosas filled his nose. That was his favorite Iftaar food. It was a deliciously flaky pastry in the shape of a triangle filled with potatoes and peas and was deep fried. It was served with two kinds of dipping sauces called chutney. One was green mint flavored, the other was brown Tamarind flavor. True lovers of samosas knew that nothing compared to the tamarind chutney.

As Isa took another deep breath to soak up the aroma of the samosas, his stomach gave out a loud growl.

"Don't worry, it's almost time to eat, Isa. You've been doing great," Baba said, patting him on the back.

Had he, though? Isa thought back at some of the choices he had made because he was hungry. And even the choice he was about to make. *What else am I supposed to do though?* Isa thought to himself. *I HAVE to sell that candy to save the carnival or we won't be able to pay for it!*

Pulling down on the straps of his backpack, Isa started to walk towards the entrance of the mosque. He needed to make sure he was seen by the adults inside the prayer hall. He didn't want them to know that hebwas going to skip Maghrib prayers to sell his candy.

Out of nowhere, Brother Hashim and Humza showed up in front of him!

Oh no, Isa thought, *I know what they are going to talk about.* Humza was avoiding eye contact and didn't really say much to Isa. *He must be annoyed about the phone call,* thought Isa. *Maybe I should say sorry.*

"Come on boys, let's go take a walk this way and check out how the carnival is looking," said Brother Hashim as he led the two boys away from the crowd entering the mosque. Isa glanced back. He needed to get into the prayer hall before the Adhaan, the call to prayer. He glanced down at his watch: 7:45 PM. He had about twenty minutes left.

"As you know, being on the cabinet of the youth committee is a pretty big responsibility," Brother Hashim began. "And you two serve as role models to many of the other kids here."

Tattletale, Isa scoffed in his head. Humza had gone and complained to Brother Hashim. Now Isa *really* didn't want to say sorry. Humza should have understood how hard fasting is! He should have understood that sometimes you say or do things you don't mean when you are hungry!

"...so you guys want to tell me why you aren't talking to each other?" Brother Hashim asked as he turned around and faced them. Isa felt awful again. Humza hadn't tattled on him.

"I'll go first," Isa offered. "I was kind of mean to Humza on the phone earlier."

"And last night at your house," added Humza with his arms crossed.

"Yeah...umm...sorry," Isa mumbled while drawing circles on the ground with his feet. There was silence as both boys stared at the ground, hoping this moment would just end.

Finally, Humza spoke. "It's okay, I know you didn't mean it. Those stomach growls really made it hard to think straight today." Isa chuckled in agreement.

"Well, I'm glad we cleared that up," said Brother Hashim, patting them both on the back.

"Now back to business; we need to go through and check on all the game booths. Humza, what time are we opening the carnival to everyone?"

"Umm...after Iftaar is served, I think," he replied.

Maybe this is my chance, Isa thought. Should he just confess now? Should he just tell them the truth? Maybe Humza would understand and not be angry.

Should Isa Confess Now? Go to page 105: The Confession	**OR**	Should he still try and sell the candy? Go to page 97: Candies for Wudu

Candies for Wudu

There was no way Humza wouldn't be mad. Isa thought how he would react if the tables were turned. He would definitely be angry with Humza and definitely stop talking to him. Isa *had* to stick to the plan. He needed to sneak away from Brother Hashim and Humza and make his appearance in the prayer hall.

"Guys, I have to go. I need to do Wudu before prayer time starts," Isa said, turning around to leave.

"Wait!" Humza called out. "Give me the money so I can pay for the prizes!"

Isa stopped in his tracks, took a breath, and continued walking away. He felt guilty, but he had no choice other than to pretend not to hear Humza. Isa looked down and practically jogged through the parking lot to the entrance of the mosque.

SLAM!

He ran smack into Sakeena and Rukaya! "Watch where you're going!" Sakeena exclaimed, adjusting her hijab. This was his chance; he needed to spread the word about his candy store.

"Oh sorry, but listen, meet me in front of the bathroom right after the Adhaan! You won't want to miss it!" Isa pitched to her.

"What are you talking about?" she asked, raising an eyebrow at him.

"Just come and you'll see," Isa said in an annoyed voice - he didn't have time to explain! "Oh, and tell everyone, just not any adults," Isa added in the end.

"Alright...but it sounds fishy. I'm assuming it's related to the youth committee?" Rukaya asked with her arms crossed.

"Yeah, yeah it is, just come okay?" Isa said, rushing past them.

He walked into the prayer hall and made his way through the crowd. He purposefully said "Salam" louder than usual so everyone would notice him and remember that he was there. Once Isa had been in the hall long enough, he slipped out and marched towards the bathroom.

His plan was to set up as soon as the Adhaan started. Kids were always late in finishing their Wudu, the washing before prayers. This way all the adults would already be lined up to pray and he wouldn't get caught. And that's when he would sell the candy to the kids - walking out of the bathroom. Isa smiled to himself. His plan felt pretty foolproof.

Quickly Isa laid out all the candy on the floor as

a display to catch everyone's attention. He leaned against the wall outside the bathroom trying to look as natural as possible. All of a sudden it felt like everyone could hear his thoughts. *Why are they looking at me?*

Isa checked his shirt to make sure nothing was on it. He was busy dusting off his pants when he felt a tap.

"Psssttt...I heard you have a kids-eyes-only thing," Zain said standing next to Isa but not looking at him. "Sakeena told me," he added.

It was working! The kids knew about his secret mission! Isa sprung into action. He wondered how many other kids would show up.

"Can I have one too?" someone asked from the other side.

"One sec," Isa responded before freezing. He recognized that voice. That wasn't a kid's voice. It was Brother Hashim's! Brother Hashim was standing there with his arms crossed with Sakeena and Humza behind him. Sakeena threw her hands up and mouthed, "I'm sorry!"

Isa turned around to try and explain when Humza showed up too. "Do you want to explain what's going on here?" Brother Hashim asked, frowning.

Isa's first instinct was to try and come up with a cover story. Scenarios were zooming in his head.

left and right. His heart was racing, and he couldn't breathe. His eyes scanned everyone's faces eagerly looking at him. His eyes paused at Humza's face. He remembered how understanding Humza had been when he finally apologized. Maybe it was time to tell the truth.

Isa explained how he was short $200 and that he was trying to raise it. "It's for a good cause!" Isa added at the end.

"So you were going to skip Maghrib prayers, and make other kids late, just so you didn't have to tell me the truth?" Humza questioned from behind Brother Hashim. Humza looked upset.
Isa looked down. He didn't know what to say anymore. He hadn't thought about it like that. "... *fasting is about being close to Allah...*" Mama's words rang in his head.

All day Isa had been so focused on his problems and how hungry he was. He hadn't really thought much about Allah at all. He remembered how calm and peaceful he felt when Baba recited the Quran and yearned to feel that again.

Taking a deep breath, he said, "I'm sorry." Isa didn't want to give an excuse or a story. He had realized what he had been doing had no excuse.

There was only silence in the air. Isa looked down; he didn't know what else he could say.

> Go to page 110

The Confession

Isa glanced back at the mosque in the distance. He saw people rushing in so they wouldn't be late for Maghrib prayer.

"...*fasting is about being closer to Allah...*" echoed Mama's words in his head.

Who was Isa kidding? His plan was never going to work. Not only did he not have enough candy to make up $200, but he had to skip Maghrib prayers to even try!

It simply wasn't worth it.

All day Isa had been so focused on his

problems and how hungry he was. He hadn't really thought much about Allah at all. He remembered how calm and peaceful he had felt when Baba recited the Quran and wanted to feel that again.

Taking a deep breath, he approached Brother Hashim and Humza.

"I have something to tell you..." Isa started. "Humza, do you remember last night when you asked me to double-check the money?"

"Yeah, it's okay, Isa, I get it. You are the treasurer and I should have trusted you," Humza replied.

"Well, actually," Isa paused and took another breath, "you were right. I should have recounted the cash."

Brother Hashim and Humza stopped in their tracks and turned around to look at Isa.

"What are you saying?" they said at the same time.

Dread was creeping back into Isa's body. He felt frozen. Moving his lips felt so hard. His throat was tight and he was pulling on his fingers so hard he thought he'd end up breaking them.

"Umm..." he tried. His heart was pounding in his chest so loudly he thought everyone could hear it. Brother Hashim walked over and put his hand on Isa's shoulder and knelt down to look at him.

"Isa, it's okay, just tell us. We are a community. We help each other," he explained.

There was no turning back now. Isa had to tell them the truth and time was running out. The Maghrib Adhaan was about to start anytime now. Isa closed his eyes and told them all about the missing $200 and how he had tried to come up with it all day.

"...and I still have the candy if we want to try and sell it. I'm so sorry," Isa concluded. His eyes were still shut. He couldn't bear to see the expressions on their faces.

There was silence. No one spoke.

They will kick me off the committee now, Isa thought to himself.

Finally, Humza spoke. "I don't get it dude, why didn't you just tell me? I would have ordered less stuff."

Isa finally opened his eyes. Humza didn't look angry. He simply looked confused. Isa had no words. He didn't know what he could possibly say to make him understand.

Just then Sakeena and Rukaya skipped over to them. They were so excited they hardly even noticed everyone's solemn faces.

"What are you guys doing here? Maghrib prayers are about to start," Sakeena said, pulling on Isa's shirt. "Humza, they are asking if you want to introduce the carnival to everyone," Rukaya said.

No one moved, and Isa closed his eyes again. *Humza is going to have to tell everyone how we won't have prizes at the carnival and it's my fault.*

Continued...

Brother Hashim broke the silence and spoke to Sakeena.

"Can you gather the ten kids who fasted for the first time today and meet me in the parking lot?"

Oh no, Isa thought. *Is Brother Hashim going to tell everyone how I messed up? This is going to be so embarrassing!*

Sakeena tried to question Brother Hashim but he simply told her to go gather the kids first. He then turned to Isa and explained his plan.

"I had planned to give each kid who fasted $20, instead I'm going to give it to the youth committee to cover the $200. I want you to talk to everyone and let them know that the carnival is all set for after Maghreb."

As Isa, Humza, and Brother Hashim walked towards the parking lot, Isa let out a sigh of relief. He was surprised how easily his problem was solved. He should have felt all the weight lifted off his shoulders, yet something was still weighing him down.

Isa stared at Br. Hashim and Humza's backs as they silently walked towards the parking lot. He should be so happy, he got exactly what he wanted. No one would ever have to know that he messed up! So why wasn't he happy? What was this new feeling that had replaced the dread.

Guilt. Isa realized that was this new feeling. The $200 that Br. Hashim gave him wasn't his, it belonged to all the kids. But he couldn't tell them the truth. It would be too embarrassing

In the parking lot, he stood in front of his friends, ready to tell them all about the carnival. Brother Hashim and Humza were looking back at him anxiously. He opened his mouth to begin and stopped.

"...*fasting is about being closer to Allah*..." echoed in Isa's head.

Isa sighed. The mosque was glowing behind the crowd of kids. How was his story going to bring him closer to Allah? He needed to have trust in Allah. He remembered Humza's confused face. He wasn't angry at Isa, just upset that Isa hadn't told him the truth.

"Guys, I messed up," Isa said, staring out at the mosque. "I messed up counting our money, and we are $200 short for the carnival. Brother Hashim was going to give us each $20 each as a reward for fasting."

And now came the hardest part. "I was wondering, would you maybe think about donating it to the carnival?" Isa said all in one breath.

"Yeah, and Isa will give you a candy as a thank you for donating!" Humza added, standing next to Isa with his arms around his shoulders.

"It's candies for a cause," Isa claimed, smiling. His heart whispered Alhumdolilah, thank you Allah. He was so blessed to have friends like Humza.

No one was moving. Isa's heart started to drop. He dropped his head and covered his face with his hands. That's when he felt a tug.

"I'll take the wafer chocolate," said Sakeena, grabbing the candy from his bag and walking away. And just like that, one by one, everyone grabbed a candy and headed to the prayer hall.

At that moment, Isa thought back to Mama's words. *"Fasting isn't just about food."* For the first time today, Isa was excited to be fasting. He finally realized, though fasting was going to be much harder than he had thought, he wasn't going to be doing it alone. He had a community that was there when things got hard.

Isa and Humza walked into the mosque just as the Adhaan began.

"Allah hu Akbar."

Meet the Author

Hira Rizvi is the founder of Zair Zabr Play - a company geared towz ards finding fun and interactive ways of introducing Islam. Some of her previous works include: My First Quran Activity Book and Names of Allah | A Memory Matching Game.

She lives in Northern California with her husband and daughter. Find out more about her on
www.zairzabrplay.com

Meet the Illustrator

Nida Syed is not only the illustrator for 'Isa's First Fast', but also the art and graphics coordinator for Kisa Kids Publications, where she's also illustrated 'Rahmah the Raindrop'. She loves to bring stories and concepts to life with art, and hopes to inspire muslims to express themselves through creativity. You can see more of her work by visiting
www.needanida.portfolio.site.